Eileen+Anita=Albert

For the Lovelorn — feathered or not.
—J. D.

*To the Shut-Eyes everywhere —
one day, love will touch you too.*
—S. F.

Text copyright © 2003 by Joyce Dunbar.
Illustrations copyright © 2003 by Sophie Fatus.

Library of Congress Cataloging-in-Publication Data Available

ISBN 0-439-47431-0

10 9 8 7 6 5 4 3 2   04 05 06 07

Printed in Singapore
Reinforced Binding for Library Use
First Orchard edition, September 2003

The L♥ve~ME BiRd

Joyce Dunbar   Sophie fatus

ORCHARD BOOKS / NEW YORK
AN IMPRINT OF SCHOLASTIC INC.

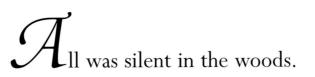

*A*ll was silent in the woods.

Suddenly, out of the green,
"Love me! Love me! Love me!" called the Love-Me bird.
There was no answer to her call.
"Love me! Love me!" the Love-Me bird trilled again.
Still, there wasn't an answer.

"Love me! Love me!" the Love-Me bird kept on
calling, until she woke up Shut-Eye, the owl.

"Some of us are trying to get some
shut-eye," grumbled Shut-Eye.
"But it's Springtime! Wing-time!
Fling-time!" said the Love-Me bird.
"Sing-a-ding-a-ling-time!"
And up she started again.

"Love me! Love me! Love me!"
But though the Love-Me bird sang all day,
and all of the next day too,
there were no answers to her call.

"There must be some birdie out there,"
she said sadly to Shut-Eye.
"Perhaps you should try another way,"
suggested Shut-Eye.
"Which way?" asked the Love-Me bird.
"Romance. Glamour. Finery and frills,"
said Shut-Eye.
"That's an idea," said the Love-Me bird.

So the Love-Me bird dressed herself up.
She plucked and primped and preened until her wings
were shaped like hearts. She brushed and dressed her crest.
She decked herself with flowers.

"Love me! Love me! Love me!" she warbled, all of a flutter.
But only the leaves fluttered back.
She warbled until she could warble no more.

"It didn't work," she said to Shut-Eye.

"Perhaps you overdid it," he replied.

"What now?" asked the Love-Me bird.

"Act helpless," said Shut-Eye,

"then a mate might come to your rescue."

So the Love-Me bird acted helpless.

With crumpled crest and drooping feathers,

she flopped around looking sorry.

"Love me. Please love me. Please," she twittered.

There came no twittering replies.

"It didn't work," she said to Shut-Eye.
"No," sighed a very tired Shut-Eye.
"Why don't you play it cool? Play hard to get."

"How do I do that?" asked the Love-Me bird.
"Stick your beak in the air and fly away,"
said Shut-Eye. "Far, far away."

So the Love-Me bird played it cool.

She stuck her beak in the air and flew far away.

But not far enough for the very sleepy Shut-Eye.

"It didn't work," she said, flying straight back.
"No-birdie knew I was hard to get."

"Perhaps you should build a nest,"
said Shut-Eye. "Another Love-Me bird might like it."
"A love-me nest," said the Love-Me bird.
"A love-each-other nest," corrected Shut-Eye.

The Love-Me bird got right to work.
She wove and spun and tweaked and threaded
until she had a fabulous nest in the sky.
She lined it with moss and feathers.
"Love me! Love me! Love me!"
she crooned from her nest.

All kinds of birds flew by.
But none of them looked at her nest.
She crooned all day and all night until
she could croon no more.

"My nest wasn't good enough,"
she said to Shut-Eye. "I'll never be loved."

"There's one last thing you can try," said Shut-Eye.

"What's that?" sniffed the Love-Me bird.

"Sing a different tune," said Shut-Eye.

"What tune?" asked the Love-Me bird.

"How about, Love you-ooo! Love you-ooo!"

Shut-Eye tu-whitted and tu-whoohed.

"But I'm a Love-*Me* bird, not a Love-*You* bird,"

said the Love-Me bird.

"Perhaps you can be both at once,"

winked Shut-Eye. "Try it and see."

The next day, all was silent in the woods until,
"Love you! Love you! Love you!"
called the Love-Me bird from her tree.

Suddenly, out of the blue . . .

"Love you! Love you! Love you!" came the answering call of another Love-Me bird.

Then there was a swoop,

and a flutter of wings . . .

. . . and at last Shut-Eye got some much needed shut-eye!